Polly and the Pirates

Tony Bradman

Illustrated by James Davies

For Joe, my piratical
grandson!
T. B.

For Mum
J. D.

EGMONT
We bring stories to life

Book Band: White

Lexile® measure: 650L

First published in Great Britain 2013
This edition published 2017
by Egmont UK Limited
The Yellow Building, 1 Nicholas Road, London W11 4AN
Text copyright © Tony Bradman 2013
Illustrations copyright © James Davies 2013
The author and illustrator have asserted their moral rights
ISBN 978 1 4052 8249 9
www.egmont.co.uk
A CIP catalogue record for this title is available from the British Library.
Printed in Singapore
52576/4

Series consultant: Nikki Gamble

CHAPTERS

Cast Adrift!

It was a cold and blustery day out on the ocean waves, and *The Jolly Herbert*'s sails flapped and snapped in the wind. But the pirates weren't taking any notice of the weather. For something far more interesting was happening . . .

Bad Bart stood on the poop deck, scowling down at Cap'n Caleb and his wife Keel-Haul Annie. The couple were surrounded by the ship's crew – the ugliest, scurviest, meanest bunch of buccaneers you ever did see, each one armed to the teeth. Annie was holding a small bundle in her arms, and scowled back.

'We'll give 'ee one last chance to end this mutiny, Bart,' Annie said.

'Aye, fair's fair,' said Caleb. 'No hard feelings if ye give in now.'

'No hard feelings? It's too late for that,' growled Bad Bart. 'The pair of 'ee should have thought how we might feel about the terrible things ye've done.'

The crew muttered and grumbled and shook their cutlasses in agreement.

'Stop talkin' bilge!' said Caleb. 'We've always been good skippers.'

'Ye were,' said Bad Bart. 'Until the day ye decided . . . *to get married*.'

'Aye, we'll never forgive 'ee for makin' us wear them there page-boy outfits,' hissed one of the men. 'And as for those hats and shoes . . . Ha!'

'Well ye didn't complain at the time,' said Annie. 'Not that ye'd have dared.'

'We might have if we'd known what horrors were to come,' growled Bad Bart. 'For after that ye did the worst thing of all. *Ye had a baby!*'

Just then a loud wailing came from Annie's bundle.

'And what a lovely baby our Polly is,' said Annie. She and Caleb beamed at their daughter.

'We don't think so,' said Bad Bart. 'She keeps us awake all night with her blasted cryin', and those nappies of hers stink even more than we do!'

'How would ye know?' said Caleb. 'Ye've never offered to change one.'

'Shiver me timbers,' groaned Bad Bart. 'We're not nursemaids, we're PIRATES! Anyhow, enough of this talkin'. I'd like to make 'ee walk the plank, but I'll settle for gettin' rid of 'ee without any fun. Put 'em in the dinghy, lads!'

The crew pushed Caleb and Annie to the

side of the ship. Caleb climbed down to the dinghy. Annie lowered Polly, then climbed down herself.

'This ain't over between us, Bart,' said Annie. 'Just ye wait and see.'

'I won't hold me breath,' laughed Bad Bart. 'Right . . . cast 'em adrift!'

The Jolly Herbert sailed on, leaving the dinghy in its wake.

Settling Down

Things looked grim for the little family. They didn't have much food and water, and they were a long way from the nearest land. But Caleb and Annie had been at sea all their lives, so they soon managed to rig a sail and set a course.

One day went past, then another. Polly gurgled away and seemed happy, and that kept her parents going. They ate the fish they caught . . . and they talked.

'I hates to say it,' muttered Caleb, 'but maybe Bart's done us a favour.'

'Ye must be jokin'!' spluttered Annie. 'Has the sun boiled your brains?'

'Think about it, my love. A pirate ship ain't really a place for a baby.'

'Ye be dead right there, Caleb,' Annie sighed. 'But what shall we do, then? Bein' pirates be the only way we know how to make a proper livin'.'

'Well, we'll have to think of somethin' else. For our Polly's sake . . .'

Just then a dark cloud covered the sun and the wind whipped up a terrible storm. The waves were like mountains, and the little dinghy was nearly swamped.

But they kept going through the night, and in the morning the sea was calmer. Caleb peered at the distant horizon. '*Land ho!*' he yelled, and they cheered.

It took them quite a while to settle down ashore. They found a house a long way inland and made it, er . . . comfortable . . .

Annie got a job handing out parking tickets (nobody ever argued with her) . . .

. . . and Caleb stayed at home to take care of Polly.

Polly grew, of course.
She learned to crawl . . .
and walk . . .

SQUAWWK!

. . . and before long
she was running . . .
and jumping . . .
and climbing. She
learned to talk as well.

'Steady as she goes!' she would say.
Or, 'Blisterin' barnacles!' Or, 'Easy on
the cornflakes, Pa, I've had my fill!' Or,
'Hooray and up she rises!' in the bath.

Shiver me
timbers, this
be fun!

'Ah, what a wonderful daughter we have,'
said Caleb one day. He and Annie were sitting
in the park, watching Polly enjoy herself on
the swings.

'Aye, things have turned out fine,' said
Annie. Then she sighed. 'Still, I'll admit to
feeling a mite bored sometimes. I do sorely
miss the pirate life.'

'Me too,' said Caleb, sighing himself. 'But Polly be fine, and that be all that do count. Look lively there, Polly – boarders on your starboard bow!'

Things never stay the same, though. Polly kept growing, of course.

Soon it was time for her to go to school . . .

Parents' Evening

Polly's teacher was called Miss Primly, and Polly thought she was wonderful. In fact, as far as Polly was concerned, Miss Primly could do no wrong. Caleb and Annie quickly got used to hearing Miss Primly's nuggets of wisdom.

'Miss Primly says you should start the day with a good breakfast,' said Polly. ('Couldn't agree more!' said Caleb.) Or: 'Miss Primly says a tidy house is the sign of a tidy mind.' ('I do like things to be shipshape meself,' said Annie.)

'Ah, she do seem a proper nice lady, does this Miss Primly,' said Caleb.

'Aye, so she do,' said Annie. 'I hope we gets the chance to meet her.'

'Your wish is granted, Ma!' said Polly. 'It's Parents' Evening tonight . . .'

The school was crowded when they got there, and they had to wait a while.

What be ye starin' at?

Some of the other parents stared at Caleb and Annie. Annie stared right back.

'It's good to meet you,' said Miss Primly. 'Polly is such a lovely girl.'

'It's kind of 'ee to say so,' said Caleb. 'But we did know that already.'

He beamed happily at Annie, and they both beamed at Miss Primly.

'Although I have to say she can sometimes be a bit loud,' said Miss Primly. 'And she does have . . . how shall I put this? An interesting turn of phrase.'

'Perishin' parrots!' said Caleb. 'Can't say I've noticed that meself.'

'We wondered how she was gettin' on with her studies,' said Annie.

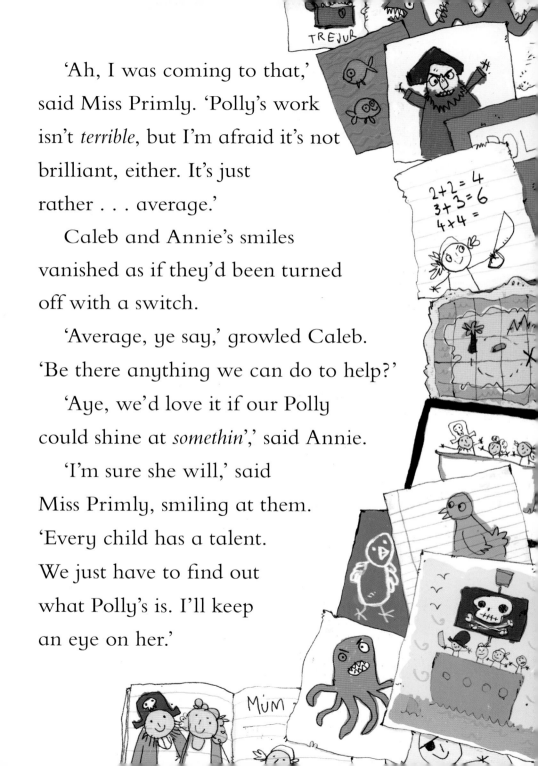

'Ah, I was coming to that,' said Miss Primly. 'Polly's work isn't *terrible*, but I'm afraid it's not brilliant, either. It's just rather . . . average.'

Caleb and Annie's smiles vanished as if they'd been turned off with a switch.

'Average, ye say,' growled Caleb. 'Be there anything we can do to help?'

'Aye, we'd love it if our Polly could shine at *somethin'*,' said Annie.

'I'm sure she will,' said Miss Primly, smiling at them. 'Every child has a talent. We just have to find out what Polly's is. I'll keep an eye on her.'

Miss Primly did just that, and discovered that Polly *was* good at some things. She could certainly climb a rope . . .

. . . and she easily won the Treasure Hunt
competition at the school fair . . . But alas, her
school work didn't improve, no matter how
much Miss Primly or Caleb and Annie tried
to help her.

Then one day Miss Primly took her class on
an outing.

Skull and Crossbones

They were going to the seaside, and Polly was *incredibly* excited.

'Miss Primly says we have to take a packed lunch and a raincoat *and* suncream,' she said. 'Miss Primly says we have to be on our best behaviour at all times. And Miss Primly says we need some parent helpers to come along . . .'

So Caleb and Annie and some of the other parents set off in the coach with Miss Primly and the children.

When they arrived,
they visited the
Sea Life Centre . . .

. . . an interesting
local museum . . .

. . . and ate their lunch
on the beach.

Then for a special treat they went for a
boat trip round the harbour.

'Ah, 'tis grand to be back at sea,' said
Caleb, taking a deep breath.

'Aye, so it is,' said Annie. 'What about it,
Polly – enjoyin' the day?'

'Yes, Ma, it's *brilliant!*' said Polly. 'But hang
on . . . what's that?'

Another ship had appeared in the harbour – a ship bristling with guns, its crew yelling and waving cutlasses. A ship flying the skull and crossbones...

'I don't believe it . . .' muttered Caleb.
'It's *The Jolly Herbert*!'

'They be headin' straight for us!' said
Annie. 'Brace yerselves!'

'Prepare to be boarded!' yelled Bad Bart, and the crew of *The Jolly Herbert* swarmed over the side of the harbour boat. Caleb and Annie tried to hold them off, and Miss Primly put up quite a fight, but it was all over pretty quickly.

'Where's Polly?' Annie whispered to Caleb as they were being tied up.

'Wish I knew,' Caleb whispered back. 'Slipped away to hide, maybe . . .'

'Stop that there whispering!' roared Bad Bart. 'Why, if it ain't old Caleb and Annie! Good to see the pair of 'ee . . . er, *not*! And this time ye can join in all the fun! Let's make 'em walk the plank!'

'You can't do that, you nasty, horrible man!' said Miss Primly.

'Shiver me timbers,' roared Bad Bart. 'I'm Bad Bart, the boldest buccaneer on the briny, and I can do whatever I want! Get her on a plank as well, lads!'

'Avast there!' a voice said suddenly. 'Step *away* from the teacher!'

Everyone stopped and looked round at a shadowy, menacing figure.

'And who be ye, then?' said Bad Bart.

The figure stepped forward.

'Me?' she said with a grin. 'I be your worst nightmare.'

Caleb and Annie couldn't believe their eyes.

POLLY!

A Proper Pirate

It *was* Polly, but she looked rather different. She wasn't wearing her school uniform or her school shoes any more, and she wasn't carrying her school bag. Instead she was dressed as a pirate from top to toe, and she carried a cutlass.

'Don't make me laugh!' growled Bad Bart. 'Ye be just a little girl!'

'Ah, that's what I might look like on the outside,' said Polly. 'But inside I'm a pirate! Sorry, Ma and Pa. I've been meanin' to tell 'ee, I've finally realised that this is what I was born to be!'

With that, Polly grabbed a
rope and swung into the attack.
She knocked over the crew
of *The Jolly Herbert* like they
were a row of skittles.
Then she chased Bad
Bart back on to *The Jolly
Herbert*, although he
wasn't so easily beaten.
'Lay on with that
there cutlass of yours
and see what it gets 'ee!'
he yelled. 'No quarter,
that's what! I'll send 'ee down
to Davy Jones's locker yet . . .'
Soon Polly and Bad Bart were having a
terrific duel. They charged all over *The Jolly
Herbert*, from the poop deck to the top of a
mast and back again.

'Shiver me timbers, shouldn't we be helping her?' said Caleb.

'No,' laughed Annie. 'She be doin' fine all by herself!'

'By golly, you're right!' said Miss Primly, her voice full of admiration. 'I do believe we've discovered what your daughter's talent is. Go for it, Polly!'

Moments later Bad Bart was on his knees, begging for mercy.

'Three cheers for our piratical Polly!' yelled

her Pa. 'Hip, hip . . . hooray!'

That's the end of the story, except to say that Polly went on to be the greatest pirate of all time. Caleb and Annie sailed with their daughter as often as they could, of course, but they also started a business with a new partner.

Teaching at *Miss Primly's Pirate Academy* was a terrific way to pass on everything they had

learned. Miss Primly learned a few things too.

As for Bad Bart, well, Caleb and Annie kept him very busy . . . with their new baby.

'Stop that snivellin', Bart!' yelled Annie. 'Just get that nappy changed!'

'Who knows?' said Caleb. 'Ye might even find ye have a talent for it . . .'

The look on Bart's face made them laugh till they cried.